McCordsville Elementary
Media Center

W9-CCA-981

Basket Moon

First Edition

Library of Congress Cataloging-in-Publication Data

Ray, Mary Lyn.
     Basket moon / by Mary Lyn Ray : illustrated by Barbara Cooney.
     — 1st ed.
          p.   cm.
     Summary: After hearing some men call his father and him hillbillies
on his first trip into the nearby town of Hudson, a young boy is not so
sure he still wants to become a basket-maker.
     ISBN 0-316-73521-3
     [1. Basket-making — Fiction.   2. Fathers and sons — Fiction.
3. Mountain life — New York (State) — Fiction.   4. New York
(State) — Fiction.]   I. Cooney, Barbara, ill.   II. Title.
PZ7.R210154Bas   1998
[E] — dc21   96-49013

                              10 9 8 7 6 5 4 3
                                       SC
                          Manufactured in China

The paintings for this book were done in oil pastel and acrylic on China silk and acetate.
                    Book design by Sheila Smallwood.

For more history of the Taghkanic basket-makers and characteristics that identify their
     work, see *Legend of the Bushwhacker Basket* (Martha Wetherbee Books, 1986).

For those who hear the wind
M. L. R.

With love to patient Maria
B. C.

Basket Moon

by Mary Lyn Ray
Illustrated by Barbara Cooney

Little, Brown and Company
Boston   New York   London

The moon was almost round. The Basket Moon.
Pa would be going to Hudson. Maybe this time
I could go, too.

It took all the days a moon grew for Pa to make a load of
baskets to take into Hudson to sell. We had no horse or
wagon, so he had to walk. And he always went when the
moon was round, to have it for a lantern if he was late
returning.

I always asked to go.

But every time he went alone. "When you're old
enough," he said, leaving me home with Ma.

The long day Pa was gone, I tried to picture Hudson. I wasn't sure what a city was. All we had for community was Big Joe and Mr. Cooens — and farther back some other families we didn't often see.

The high land where we lived was poor land, no good for growing crops. But it grew basket trees. Black ash, white oak, hickory, maple. I knew already that black ash was best for baskets. I knew how to tell ash leaves from maple and pine and oak. I knew from Pa.

He told Big Joe and Mr. Cooens I was a watcher. I
could tell it pleased him.

I watched how the men cut the trees and sawed them
into logs, which they carried home on their shoulders.

I watched how they pounded the logs with mallets to
free the splint ribbons.

When Pa started a basket bottom, he laid the splint in a great round sun. Then he bent the ribs to shape the sides and began to weave. Under, over. Under, over.

When the bowl of a basket was done, Pa rimmed it — with splint thick as a sapling, curled around the top. Then he put on a handle. He took a stick and smoothed it and bent it across the basket. At each end he whittled tails, which he slipped into the side and locked around the rim. He laced the last splint tight. Then he handed me the basket to take to the basket shed. And he started a new bottom.

Now the shed was full. And the moon almost. Would Pa say yes this time?

I was eight. I knew the green damp, dark smells that bloomed on the hill. I could track the places where black ash grew. Eight must be old enough.

But Pa gave the answer he always gave.

So I went back to watching and waiting for another Basket Moon. Orange and yellow blew from the trees. In summer the men worked in the shade of these trees. Now they came into the kitchen by the stove.

Dark settled and talk settled as they sat making baskets. Sometimes Pa spoke, sometimes Big Joe or Mr. Cooens. They told and retold stories they said the trees told them.

I wanted to hear trees talk, too. But I heard nothing when I listened to the night.

The fire sputtered. A chair shifted. Splint slapped the floor.

Big Joe said, "Ears that listen are ears that hear."

I wasn't sure I understood what he was saying. But I knew it meant more waiting.

I was used to waiting.

I listened to snow fall. I listened to ice drip and melt. I listened to buds unwrap their leaves. But I couldn't hear trees talk. And when Pa went to Hudson, he still left me home with Ma — even though I was eight and a half.

Green light came back to the trees, where even the sun seemed green under their branches. I helped peel splint. Pa let me try some weaving. Under. Over. Under. Over.

Then I had a birthday. I was nine. Soon after, I began to see Pa studying me the way he checked a basket when it was finished. He didn't say what he was thinking. But when a week or two went by, and the moon was round again, and Pa was packing up for Hudson, he said, "I reckon you could come."

Ma made us lunch and helped us string the baskets onto poles we carried across our shoulders. She said all anyone would see was a bunch of baskets bumping down the road.

Once off the hill, the road was flat. It took us by an orchard with six hundred apple trees. I counted so I could tell Ma. Or I counted fifty and guessed the rest. The road took us by stone houses with square yards and gardens. It took us by big farms. The land lay wide and open. As we walked, the baskets danced.

Then the dirt road turned into pavement: Hudson!

Suddenly there were many streets. But Pa seemed to know them. We went to Janssen's Hardware. Here were shelves of pans and pails, stovepipe, dishes plain and painted, saw blades, bean pots, snowshoes, oil lamps, fishing nets, hunting vests, pocketknives, felt hats, grapple hooks, stoneware crocks.

Pa piled the baskets on the counter. The green smell that stayed in them became part of the store smell — kerosene

and leather and nails in metal bins. I watched Pa trade our baskets for what we needed.

Then we went to Luyckman's Grocery to buy what Ma was wanting. Graham flour, white flour, baking powder, ginger, raisins, lemons, lard, pea beans, onions, canned tomatoes . . .

The colors made me stare: the printed labels on the cans, fruits and vegetables in careful rows, the great blond cheese, pink soda, white eggs.

Hudson smelled of brick and business.

But it also held a musty smell, a smell of river and
ships. Which we followed to the water, where Pa bought
bananas right off a boat. Then he hitched them to a
basket pole, with the other things we'd bought, and we
started the long walk home.

Back through the streets, back by the stores, I was thinking how to tell Ma about Hudson — when, across the square, a man called out, "A tisket, a tasket, hillbilly basket! That's all a bushwhacker knows."

I turned to look. The man laughed, and the men around him laughed. Pa said to pay no mind. It was something he had heard before.

But I felt a shadow all the way home. CAW, CAW, CAW. Their laughter seemed to circle like crows.

Ma had the lamps lit and was making pancakes for our supper. But I didn't want to eat.

When I told her what had happened, she said, "The trees know what we know. Doesn't much matter if some folk in Hudson don't."

I wanted to tell her it mattered to me.

Next morning, Pa went on making baskets. But I felt no pleasure watching. The pleasure was gone from tracking ash. Pulling splint. Smelling splint. Stacking baskets in the shed. Baskets were nothing to be proud of. Hillbillies made baskets.

I'd never go to Hudson again. And I didn't want Pa to go back.

For several weeks I watched for a day when I knew where Ma was, where Pa was, where Mr. Cooens and Big Joe were. Then I opened the basket shed.

I kicked the columns tall as stems of trees. "A tisket, a tasket." The baskets fell. But they wouldn't break. Pa made good baskets.

I didn't see Big Joe coming around the yard. "Needed some splint," he said. But we both knew he didn't.

Big Joe stood in the mess of baskets. For a long time he was silent, and I copied his silence. Then he began to pick the baskets up and put them back in stacks.

"Some learn the language of the wind," he said, "and sing it into music. Some hear it and write poems. The wind taught us to weave it into baskets."

An oak leaf blew into the shed. "The wind watches," Big Joe said. "It knows whom to trust."

Right then, I didn't care about the men in Hudson. I wanted to be like Big Joe and Mr. Cooens and Pa. I wanted to be one the wind chose.

I went into the woods and listened. I returned to the shed and listened. I held damp splint and listened. But I heard nothing. I picked up strips from the chips and scraps and made a little sun like the sun Pa made to start a bottom. And I began to braid. Under and over. Under and over. Still I heard nothing.

But in the night, when the stove was quiet, and the house was quiet, I heard the wind call. "Come."

I followed. Under, over. Under and over the night limbs, the dark limbs, where the wind wove.

In the half-light of the half-woven moon, every leaf seemed to salute me.

In the morning, branches rubbing against the house woke me. "Trees are stretching," Ma said. "Growing splint. Growing baskets."

I knew.

The baskets they were growing were baskets I would make.

The wind had called my name.

Author's Note

For more than a hundred years, not far from Hudson, New York, a maze of families scattered in the highlands of Columbia County made a living — and made art — making baskets. Periodically they appeared in towns around the county with baskets to sell. That was all people of the Taconic area knew about them. But parents warned their children against the "bushwhackers." The woods where they lived seemed spooked to outsiders. Stories grew. And myth was near already. To the west was the spine of the Catskills, where Rip Van Winkle slept and the headless horseman rode.

By 1900 no one remembered when this community had developed. Even the basket-makers knew only that they had been there a long time and that for a long time they had been making baskets. They made thousands. By the 1950s, however, baskets were being replaced by paper bags, cardboard boxes, and plastic. Few collectors were thinking yet of baskets. There were fewer black ash trees to make baskets from. So fewer and fewer families made baskets. But some continued. And until her death in 1996, a remaining basket-maker was still making these same baskets.

The round, brown baskets the basket-makers made are classic baskets, some of the best ever made by any basket-maker anywhere. Many survive: in museums, in barns, in collections of American folk art. They were made to last.